Text & illustrations © 2012 Éditions Milan
Translation © 2014 Sarah Quinn

Published in North America in 2014 by Owlkids Books Inc.

Published in France under the title *Supercoquet* in 2012 by Éditions Milan.

Owlkids Books acknowledges the financial support of the Canada Council for the Arts, the Ontario Arts Council, the Government of Canada through the Canada Book Fund (CBF) and the Government of Ontario through the Ontario Media Development Corporation's Book Initiative for our publishing activities.

Published in Canada by
Owlkids Books Inc.
10 Lower Spadina Avenue
Toronto, ON M5V 2Z2

Published in the United States by
Owlkids Books Inc.
1700 Fourth Street
Berkeley, CA 94710

Library and Archives Canada Cataloguing in Publication

Delaporte, Bérengère, 1979- [Super coquet. English]
    Superfab saves the day / text by Bérengère Delaporte and Jean Leroy ; illustrations by Bérengère Delaporte.

Translation of: Super coquet.
ISBN 978-1-77147-076-6 (bound)

    I. Leroy, Jean, 1975-, author II. Title. III. Title: Super coquet. English

PZ7.D4373Sup 2014   j843'.92   C2014-900170-3

Library of Congress Control Number: 2014931868

Manufactured in Shenzhen, China, in March 2014, by C&C Joint Printing Co.
Job #HO0175

A   B   C   D   E   F

 Publisher of Chirp, chickaDEE and OWL
www.owlkidsbooks.com

SUPERFAB
SAVES THE DAY

For SuperSégo, my Supersister. — B.D.

Text by Bérengère Delaporte and Jean Leroy
Illustrations by Bérengère Delaporte

SUPERFAB
SAVES THE DAY

Owl kids

Superfab was really SUPER.
He lived in a SUPER rabbit hole with a SUPER living room, where
he read SUPER books.
He even had a SUPER kitchen, where he made his SUPER-spicy
pumpkin-carrot soup.
But, best of all, Superfab's SUPER rabbit hole had...

...a SUPER walk-in closet!

"Hmmm, what should I wear today?"

"Nope, too old!"
"That's totally out of style!"
"No way! I can't go out looking like this—
they'll call me Supercarrot for sure!"

Being the best-dressed superhero sure took a long time.
So long that...

...by the time Superfab finally arrived at the scene of a crime, another superhero with a super costume would have already gotten the job done.

Everyone got tired of Superfab always being late.
They called him less and less, and then they stopped calling him at all.

Superfab became super-sad.

Then, one day, the red phone rang again.

"Humph. It must be a wrong number!"
Superfab thought to himself.

But a voice shouted over the phone, "Help, Superfab! A monster is attacking the city, and he won't leave until it is completely destroyed!"

"Finally!" thought Superfab. "Justice and good taste are going to save the day!"

Superfab wanted to be SUPER efficient, so he only changed his costume
three times before heading out. He made it downtown in less than an hour.

"A new record!" he cried.

It didn't take Superfab long to figure out why he'd been called. It seemed that he was the only superhero left who could still put up a fight!

With his heart in his throat, Superfab courageously marched up to the huge creature, whose back was turned to him.

"Hey, you! Hey...uhhh...you big lump!"

"Wow! Those are SUPER gloves! Where did you get them?" the monster asked.

"I made them myself!" Superfab replied.

"I want them! Hand them over!"

"Hmmm, I don't know...I stayed up a few nights in a row to make these gloves. It took forever to design the pattern, choose the fabric, stitch them together..."

"Please, I'm begging you—I just have to have those gloves!"

"Well, okay...on one condition."

"What's that?"

"You must leave our planet right away!"

"That's impossible! I am the Destroyer! I can't leave until everything is destroyed!"

"Oh, well, I guess you're out of luck."

Superfab took off one of his gloves and pretended
to chew on one of the fingers.

Immediately, the monster shouted, "Please, no!
Stop! I'll do whatever you want!"

As soon as the Destroyer's ship had disappeared into space, everyone came to congratulate Superfab, the superhero who had defeated a giant just by removing a glove.

When he got home, Superfab reached for his SUPER cellphone...

The Destroyer's surprised face filled the screen.

Superfab asked him excitedly, "Where did you get your SUPER hood?
It's so retro!"

"My mom made it for me!" the monster replied proudly.
"Would you like her number?"

"Yes, please! That would be SUPER!"

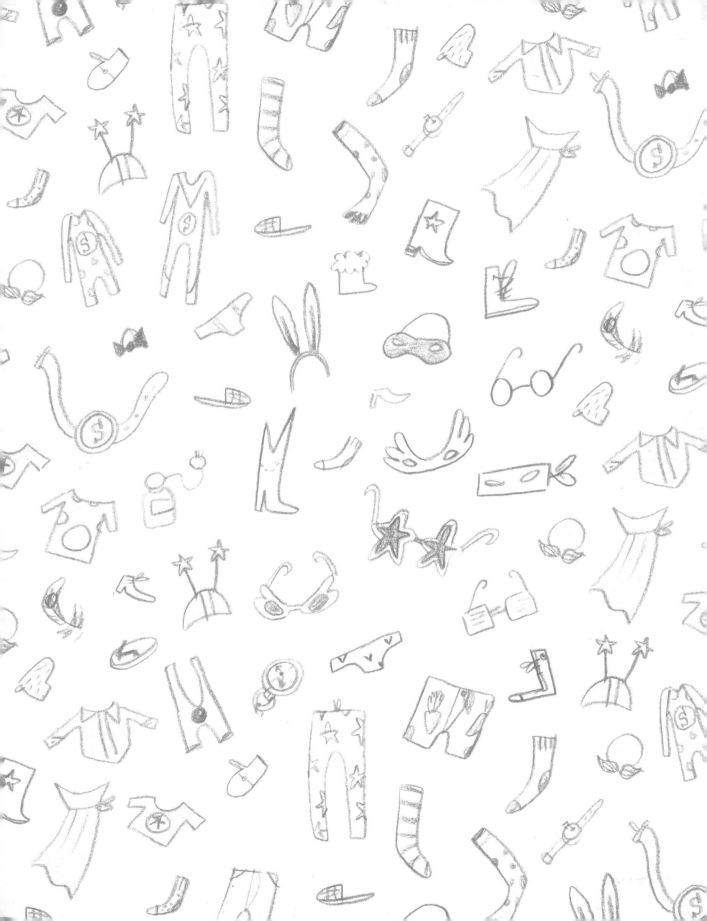